Apex Magazine

2015 Sampler

Jason Sizemore, Editor-in-Chief

Apex Magazine is a monthly digital e-zine of professional-level science fiction, fantasy, and horror short fiction.

Subscriptions of nicely formatted DRM-free eBook editions of the magazine are available. Alternatively, most content can be found at Apex-Magazine.com.

Enjoy this small sampling of what we offer to our readers.

www.apex-magazine.com

Apex Magazine 2015 Sampler © 2016 by Jason Sizemore.

ISBN: 978-1-937009-42-7

Cover Art © Matt Davis

Title Design by Justin Stewart

Published by Apex Publications, LLC
PO Box 24323
Lexington, KY 40524

TABLE OF CONTENTS

POCOSIN

Ursula Vernon

Author's Note: Pocosins are a type of raised peat wetland found almost exclusively in the Carolinas. The name derives from an Eastern Algonquian word meaning "swamp on a hill."

They are a rare and unique ecosystem, today widely threatened by development.

This is the place of the carnivores, the pool ringed with sundews and the fat funnels of the pitcher plants.

This is the place where the ground never dries out and the loblolly pines grow stunted, where the soil is poor and the plants turn to other means of feeding themselves.

This is the place where the hairstreak butterflies flow sleekly through the air and you can hear insect feet drumming inside the bowl of the pitcher plants.

This is the place where the old god came to die.

He came in the shape of the least of all creatures, a possum. Sometimes he was a man with a long rat's tail, and sometimes he was a possum with too-human hands. On two legs and four, staggering, with his hands full of mud, he came limping through the marsh and crawled up to the witchwoman's porch.

"Go back," she said, not looking up. She had a rocking chair on the porch and the runners creaked as she rocked. There was a second chair, but she did not offer it to him. "Go back where you came from."

The old god laid his head on the lowest step. When he breathed, it hissed through his long possum teeth and sounded like he was dying.

"I'm done with that sort of thing," she said, still not looking up. She was tying flies, a pleasantly tricky bit of work, binding thread and chicken feathers to the wickedness of the hook. "You go find some other woman with witchblood in her."

The old god shuddered and then he was mostly a man. He crawled up two steps and sagged onto the porch.

The woman sighed and set her work aside. "Don't try to tell me you're dying," she said grimly. "I won't believe it. Not from a possum."

Her name was Maggie Grey. She was not so very old, perhaps, but she had the kind of spirit that is born old and grows cynical. She looked down on the scruffy rat-tailed god with irritation and a growing sense of duty.

His throat rasped as he swallowed. He reached out a hand with long yellow nails and pawed at the boards on the porch.

"Shit," Maggie said finally, and went inside to get some water.

She poured it down his throat and most of it went down. He came a little bit more alive and looked at her with huge, dark eyes. His face was dirty pale, his hair iron gray.

She knew perfectly well what he was. Witchblood isn't the same as godblood, but they know each other when they meet in the street. The question was why a god had decided to die on her porch, and that was a lousy sort of question.

"You ain't been shot," she said. "There's not a hunter alive that could shoot the likes of you. What's got you dragging your sorry ass up on my porch, old god?"

The old god heaved himself farther up on the porch. He smelled rank. His fur was matted with urine when he was a possum and his pants were stained and crusted when he was a man.

His left leg was swollen at the knee, a fat bent sausage, and the foot beneath it was black. There were puncture wounds in his skin. Maggie grunted.

"Cottonmouth, was it?"

The old god nodded.

Maggie sat back down in the rocking chair and looked out over the sundew pool.

There was a dense mat of shrubs all around the house, fetterbush and sheep laurel bound up together with greenbrier. She kept the path open with an axe, when she bothered to keep it open at all. There was no one to see her and the dying man who wasn't quite a man.

Mosquitos whined in the throats of the pitcher plants and circled the possum god's head. Maggie could feel her shoulders starting to tense up. It was always her shoulders. On a bad day, they'd get so knotted that pain would shoot down her forearms in bright white lines.

"Would've preferred a deer," she said. "Or a bear, maybe. Got some dignity that way." Then she laughed. "Should've figured I'd get a possum. It'd be a nasty, stinking sort of god that wanted anything to do with me."

She picked up a pair of scissors from where she'd been tying flies. "Hold still. No, I ain't gonna cut you. I ain't so far gone to try and suck the poison out of a god."

It had likely been another god that poisoned him, she thought—Old

Lady Cottonmouth, with her gums as white as wedding veils. She saw them sometimes, big, heavy-bodied snakes, gliding easy through the water. Hadn't ever seen the Old Lady, but she was out there, and it would be just like a possum to freeze up when those white gums came at him, sprouting up fangs.

Even a witch might hesitate at that.

She waited until he was a man, more or less, and cut his pant leg open with the scissors. The flesh underneath was angry red, scored with purple. He gasped in relief as the tight cloth fell away from the swollen flesh.

"Don't thank me," she said grimly. "Probably took a few hours off your life with that. But they wouldn't be anything worth hanging on for."

She brought him more water. The first frogs began to screek and squeal in the water.

"You sure you want this?" she asked. "I can put a knife across your throat, make it easy."

He shook his head.

"You know who's coming for you?"

He nodded. Then he was a possum again and he gaped his mouth open and hissed in pain.

She hesitated, still holding the scissors. "Ain't sure I want to deal with 'em myself," she muttered. "I'm done with all that. I came out here to get away, you hear me?"

The possum closed his eyes, and whispered the only word he'd ever speak.

"...sorry..."

Maggie thrust the scissors into her pocket and scowled.

"All right," she said. "Let's get you under the porch. You come to me and I'll stand them off for you, right enough, but you better not be in plain sight."

She had to carry him down the steps. His bad leg would take no weight and he fell against her, smelling rank. There were long stains on her clothes before they were done.

Under the porch, it was cool. The whole house was raised up, to save it from the spring floods, when the sundew pool reached out hungry arms. There was space enough, in the shadow under the stairs, for a dying god smaller than a man.

She didn't need to tell him to stay quiet.

She went into the house and poured herself a drink. The alcohol was sharp and raw on her throat. She went down the steps again, to a low green stand of mountain mint, and yanked up a half dozen stems.

They didn't gentle the alcohol, but at least it gave her something else to taste. The frogs got louder and the shadows under the sheep laurel got thick.

Maggie sat back in her rocking chair with her shoulders knotting up under her shirt and went back to tying flies.

Someone cleared his throat.

She glanced up, and there was a man in preacher's clothes, with the white collar and clean black pants. The crease in them was pressed sharp enough to draw blood.

"Huh," she said. "Figured the other one'd beat you here."

He gave her a pained, fatherly smile.

She nodded to the other chair. "Have a seat. I've got bad whiskey, but if you cut it with mint and sugar, it ain't bad."

"No, thank you," said the preacher. He sat down on the edge of the chair. His skin was peat colored and there was no mud on his shoes. "You know why I've come, Margaret."

"Maggie," she said. "My mother's the only one who calls me Margaret, and she's dead, as you very well know."

The preacher tilted his head in acknowledgment.

He was waiting for her to say something, but it's the nature of witches to outwait God if they can, and the nature of God to forgive poor sinners their pride. Eventually he said, "There's a poor lost soul under your porch, Maggie Grey."

"He didn't seem so lost," she said. "He walked here under his own power."

"All souls are lost without me," said the preacher.

Maggie rolled her eyes.

A whip-poor-will called, placing the notes end to end, whip-er-will! whip-er-will!

It was probably Maggie's imagination that she could hear the panting of the god under the porch, in time to the nightjar's calls.

The preacher sat, in perfect patience, with his wrists on his knees. The mosquitos that formed skittering sheets over the pond did not approach him.

"What's there for a possum in heaven, anyway?" asked Maggie. "You gonna fill up the corners with compost bins and rotten fruit?"

The preacher laughed. He had a gorgeous, church-organ laugh and Maggie's heart clenched like a fist in her chest at the sound. She told her heart to behave. Witchblood ought to know better than to hold out hope of heaven.

"I could," said the preacher. "Would you give him to me if I did?"

Maggie shook her head.

His voice dropped, a father explaining the world to a child. "What good does it do him, to be trapped in this world? What good does it do anyone?"

"He seems to like it."

"He is a prisoner of this place. Give him to me and I will set him free to glory."

"He's a possum," said Maggie tartly. "He ain't got much use for glory."

The preacher exhaled. It was most notable because, until then, he hadn't been breathing. "You cannot doubt my word, my child."

"I ain't doubting nothing," said Maggie. "It'd be just exactly as you said, I bet. But he came to me because that's not what he wanted, and I ain't taking that away from him."

The preacher sighed. It was a more-in-sorrow-than-in-anger sigh, and Maggie narrowed her eyes. Her heart went back to acting the way a witch's heart ought to act, which was generally to ache at every damn thing and carry on anyway. Her shoulders felt like she'd been hauling stones.

"I could change your mind," he offered.

"Ain't your way."

He sighed again.

"Should've sent one of the saints," said Maggie, taking pity on the Lord, or whatever little piece of Him was sitting on her porch. "Somebody who was alive once, anyway, and remembers what it was like."

He bowed his head. "I will forgive you," he said.

"I know you will," said Maggie kindly. "Now get gone before the other one shows up."

Her voice sounded as if she shooed the Lord off her porch every day, and when she looked up again, he was gone.

It got dark. The stars came out, one by one, and were reflected in the sundew pool. Fireflies jittered, but only a few. Fireflies like grass and open woods, and the dense mat of the swamp did not please them. Maggie lit a lamp to tie flies by.

The Devil came up through a stand of yellowroot, stepping up out of the ground like a man climbing a staircase. Maggie was pleased to see that he had split hooves. She would have been terribly disappointed if he'd been wearing shoes.

He kicked aside the sticks of yellowroot, tearing shreds off them, showing ochre-colored pith underneath. Maggie raised an eyebrow at this small destruction, but yellowroot is hard to kill.

"Maggie Grey," said the fellow they called the Old Gentleman.

She nodded to him, and he took it as invitation, dancing up the steps on clacking hooves. Maggie smiled a little as he came up the steps, for the Devil always was a good dancer.

He sat down in the same chair that the preacher had used, and scowled abruptly. "See I got here late."

"Looks that way," said Maggie Grey.

He dug his shoulder blades into the back of the chair, first one, then the other, rolling a little, like a cat marking territory in something foul. Maggie stifled a sigh. It had been a good rocking chair, but it probably wasn't wise to keep a chair around that the Devil had claimed.

"You've got something I want, Maggie Grey," he said.

"If it's my soul, you'll be waiting awhile," said Maggie, holding up a bit of feather. She looped three black threads around it, splitting the feather so it looked like wings. The hook gleamed between her fingers.

"Oh no," said the Devil, "I know better than to mess with a witch's soul, Maggie Grey. One of my devils showed up to tempt your great-grandmother, and she bit him in half and threw his horns down the well."

Maggie sniffed. "Well's gone dry," she said, trying not to look pleased. She knew better than to respond to demonic flattery. "It's the ground hereabouts. Sand and moss and swamps on top of hills. Had to dig another one, and lord knows how long it'll last."

"Didn't come here to discuss well-digging, Maggie Grey."

"I suppose not." She bit off a thread.

"There's an old god dying under your porch, Maggie Grey. The fellow upstairs wants him, and I aim to take him instead."

She sighed. A firefly wandered into a pitcher plant and stayed, pulsing green through the thin flesh. "What do you lot want with a scrawny old possum god, anyway?"

The Devil propped his chin on his hand. He was handsome, of course. It would have offended his notion of his own craftsmanship to be anything less. "Me? Not much. The fellow upstairs wants him because he's a stray bit from back before he and I were feuding. An old loose end, if you follow me."

Maggie snorted. "Loose end? The possum gods and the deer and Old Lady Cottonmouth were here before anybody thought to worship you. Either of you."

The Devil smiled. "Can't imagine there's many worshippers left for an old possum god, either. 'Cept the possums, and they don't go to church much."

Maggie bent her head over the wisp of thread and metal. "He doesn't feel like leaving."

Her guest sat up a little straighter. "I am not sure," he said, silky-voiced, "that he is strong enough to stop me."

Maggie picked up the pliers and bent the hook, just a little, working the feathers onto it. "He dies all the time," she said calmly. "You never picked him up the other times."

"Can only die so many times, Maggie Grey. Starts to take it out of you.

Starts to make you tired, right down to the center of your bones. You know what that's like, don't you?"

She did not respond, because the worst thing you can do is let the Devil know when he's struck home.

"He's weak now and dying slow. Easy pickings."

"Seems like I might object," she said quietly.

The Devil stood up. He was very tall and he threw a shadow clear over the pool when he stood. The sundews folded their sticky leaves in where the shadow touched them. Under the porch steps, the dying god moaned.

He placed a hand on the back of her chair and leaned over her.

"We can make this easy, Maggie Grey," he said. "Or we can make it very hard."

She nodded slowly, gazing over the sundew pool.

"Come on—" the Devil began, and Maggie moved like Old Lady Cottonmouth and slammed the fish-hook over her shoulder and into the hand on the back of her chair.

The Devil let out a yelp like a kicked dog and staggered backwards.

"You come to my house," snapped Maggie, thrusting the pliers at him, "and you have the nerve to threaten me? A witch in her own home? I'll shoe your hooves in holy iron and throw you down the well, you hear me?"

"Holy iron won't be kind to witchblood," he gasped, doubled over.

"It'll be a lot less kind to you," she growled.

The Devil looked at his hand, with the fish-hook buried in the meat of his palm, and gave a short, breathless laugh. "Oh, Maggie Grey," he said, straightening up. "You aren't the woman your great-grandmother was, but you're not far off."

"Get gone," said Maggie. "Get gone and don't come back unless I call."

"You will eventually," he said.

"Maybe so. But not today."

He gave her a little salute, with the hook still stuck in his hand, and limped off the porch. The yellowroot rustled as he sank into the dirt again.

His blood left black spots on the earth. She picked up the lantern and went to peer at the possum god.

He was still alive, though almost all possum now. His whiskers lay limp and stained with yellow. There was white all around his eyes and a black crust of blood over his hind leg.

"Not much longer," she said. "Only one more to go, and then it's over. And we'll both be glad."

He nodded, closing his eyes.

On the way back onto the porch, she kicked at a black bloodstain, which had sprouted a little green rosette of leaves. A white flower coiled out of the leaves and turned its face to the moon.

"Bindweed," she muttered. "Lovely. One more damn chore tomorrow."

She stomped back onto the porch and poured another finger of whiskey.

It was almost midnight when the wind slowed, and the singing frogs fell silent, one by one.

Maggie looked over, and Death was sitting in the rocking chair.

"Grandmother," she said. "I figured you'd come."

"Always," said Death.

"If you'd come a little sooner, would've saved me some trouble."

Death laughed. She was a short, round woman with hair as gray as Maggie's own. "Seems to me you were equal to it."

Maggie grunted. "Whiskey?"

"Thank you."

They sat together on the porch, drinking. Death's rocker squeaked in time to the breathing of the dying god.

"I hate this," said Maggie, to no one in particular. "I'm tired, you hear me? I'm tired of all these fights. I'm tired of taking care of things, over and over, and having to do it again the next day." She glared over the top of her whiskey. "And don't tell me that it does make a difference, because I know that, too. Ain't I a witch?"

Death smiled. "Wouldn't dream of it," she said.

Maggie snorted.

After a minute, she said, "I'm so damn tired of stupid."

Death laughed out loud, a clear sound that rang over the water. "Aren't we all?" she said. "Gods and devils, aren't we all?"

The frogs had stopped. So had the crickets. One whip-poor-will sang uncertainly, off on the other side of the pond. It was quiet and peaceful and it would have been a lovely night, if the smell of the dying possum hadn't come creeping up from under the porch.

Death gazed into her mug, where the wilting mint was losing the fight against the whiskey. "Can't fix stupid," she said. "But other things, maybe. You feeling like dying?"

Maggie sighed. It wasn't a temptation, even with her shoulders sending bright sparks of pain toward her fingers and making the pliers hard to hold steady. "Feeling like resting," she said. "For a couple of months, at least. That's all I want. Just a little bit of time to sit here and tie flies and drink whiskey and let somebody else fight the hard fights."

Death nodded. "So take it," she said. "Nobody's gonna give it to you."

Maggie scowled. "I was," she said bitterly. "'Til a possum god showed up to die."

Death laughed. "It's why he came, you know," she said. Her eyes twinkled, just like Maggie's grandmother's had when she wore the body that Death was wearing now. "He wanted to be left alone to die, so he found a witch that'd understand."

Maggie raked her fingers through her hair. "Son of a bitch," she said to no one in particular.

Death finished her drink and set it aside. "Shall we do what's needful?"

Maggie slugged down the rest of the mug and gasped as the whiskey burned down her throat. "Needful," she said thickly. "That's being a witch for you."

"No," said Death, "that's being alive. Being a witch just means the things that need doing are bigger."

They went down the stairs. The boards creaked under Maggie's feet, but not under Death's, even though Death had heavy boots on.

Maggie crouched down and said, "She's here for you, hon."

She would have sworn that the possum had no strength left in him, but he crawled out from under the porch, hand over hand. His hind legs dragged and his tail looked like a dead worm.

There was nothing noble about him. He stank and black fluid leaked from his ears and the corners of his eyes. Even now, Maggie could hardly believe that God and the Devil would both show up to bargain for such a creature's soul.

Death knelt down, heedless of the smell and the damp, and held out her arms.

The possum god crawled the last little way and fell into her embrace.

"There you are," said Death, laying her cheek on the spikey-furred forehead. "There you are. I've got you."

The god closed his eyes. His breath went out on a long, long sigh, and he did not draw another one.

Maggie walked away, to the edge of the sundew pool, and waited.

A frog started up, then another one. The water rippled as their throat sacs swelled. Something splashed out in the dark.

"It's done," called Death, and Maggie turned back.

The god looks smaller now. Death had gathered him up and he almost fit in her lap, like a small child or a large dog.

"Don't suppose he's faking it?" asked Maggie hopefully. "They're famous for it, after all."

Death shook her head. "Even possum gods got to die sometime. Help me get him into the pond."

Maggie took him under the arms and Death took the feet. His tail dragged on the ground as they hauled him. Death went into the water first, sure-footed, and Maggie followed, feeling water come in over the tops of her shoes.

"If I'd been thinking, I would've worn waders," she said.

Death laughed Maggie's grandmother's laugh.

The bottom of the sundew pool was made of mud and sphagnum moss, and it wasn't always sure if it wanted to be solid or not. Every step she took required a pause while the mud settled and sometimes her heels sank in deep. She started to worry that she was going to lose her shoes in the pool, and god, wouldn't that be a bitch on top of everything else?

At least the god floated. Her shoulders weren't up to much more than that.

In the middle of the pool, Death stopped. She let go of the possum's feet and came around to Maggie's side. "This ought to do it," she said.

"If we leave the body in here, it'll stink up the pool something fierce," said Maggie. "There's things that come and drink here."

"Won't be a problem," Death promised. She paused. "Thought you were tired of taking care of things?"

"I am," snapped Maggie. "Tired isn't the same as can't. Though if this keeps up..."

She trailed off because she truly did not know what lay at the end of being tired and it was starting to scare her a little.

Death took the possum's head between her hands. Maggie put a hand in the center of his chest.

They pushed him under the water and held him for the space of a dozen heartbeats, then brought him to the surface.

"Again," said Death.

They dunked him again.

"Three times the charm," said Death, and they pushed him under the final time.

The body seemed to melt away under Maggie's hands. One moment it was a solid, hairy weight, then it wasn't. For a moment she thought it was sinking and her heart sank with it, because fishing a dead god out of the pond was going to be a bitch of a way to spend an hour.

But he did not sink. Instead he simply unmade himself, skin from flesh and flesh from bone, unraveling like one of her flies coming untied, and there was nothing left but a shadow on the surface of the water.

Maggie let out a breath and scrubbed her hands together. They felt oily.

She was freezing and her boots were full of water and something slimy wiggled past her shin. She sighed. It seemed, as it had for a long time, that witchcraft—or whatever this was—was all mud and death and need.

She was so damn tired.

She thought perhaps she'd cry, and then she thought that wouldn't much help, so she didn't.

Death reached out and took her granddaughter's hand.

"Look," said Death quietly.

Around the pond, the fat trumpets of the pitcher plants began to glow from inside, as if they had swallowed a thousand fireflies. The light cast green shadows across the surface of the water and turned the sundews into strings of cut glass beads. It cut itself along the leaves of the staggerbush and threaded between the fly-traps' teeth.

Whatever was left of the possum god glowed like foxfire.

Hand in hand, they came ashore by pitcher plant light.

Death stood at the foot of the steps. Maggie went up them, holding the railing, moving slow.

There were black stains on the steps where the god had oozed. She was going to have to scrub them down, pour bleach on them, maybe even strip the wood. The bindweed, that nasty little plant they called "Devil's Guts," was already several feet long and headed toward the mint patch. The stink of dying possum was coming up from under the steps and that was going to need to be scraped down with a shovel and then powdered with lime.

At least she could wait until tomorrow to take an axe to the Devil's rocking chair, though it might be sensible to drag it off the porch first.

The notion of all the work to be done made her head throb and her shoulders climb toward her ears.

"Go to bed, granddaughter," said Death kindly. "Take your rest. The world can go on without you for a little while."

"Work to be done," Maggie muttered. She held onto the railing to stop from swaying.

"Yes," said Death, "but not by you. Not tonight. I will make you this little bargain, granddaughter, in recognition of a kindness. I will give you a little time. Go to sleep. Things left undone will be no worse for it."

Death makes bargains rarely, and unlike the Devil, hers are not negotiable. Maggie nodded and went inside.

She fell straight down on the bed and was asleep without taking off her boots. She did not say goodbye to the being that wore her grandmother's face, but in the morning, a quilt had been pulled up over her shoulder.

The next evening, as the sun set, Maggie sat in her rocking chair and tied flies. Her shoulders were slowly, slowly easing. The pliers only shook a little in her hand.

She had dumped bleach over the steps, and the smell from under the porch had gone of its own accord. The bindweed...well, the black husks had definitely been bindweed, but something had trod upon it and turned it into ash. It was a kindness she hadn't expected.

Her whiskey bottle was also full, with something rather better than moonshine, although she suspected that a certain cloven-hooved gentleman might have been responsible for that.

The space on the porch where the other rocking chair had been ached like a sore tooth and caught her eye whenever she glanced over. She sighed. Still, the wood would keep the fire going for a couple of days, when winter came.

The throats of the pitcher plants still glowed, just a little. Easy enough to blame on tired eyes. Maggie wrapped thread around the puff of feather and the shining metal hook, and watched the glow from the corner of her eyes.

A young possum trundled out of the thicket, and Maggie looked up.

"Don't start," she said warningly. "I'll get the broom."

The possum sat down on the edge of the pond. It was an awkward, ungainly little creature, with big dark eyes and wicked kinked whiskers. It was halfway hideous and halfway sweet, which gave it something in common with witches.

Slowly, slowly, the moon rose and the green light died away. The frogs chanted together in the dark.

The possum stood up, stretched, and nodded once to Maggie Grey. Then it shuffled into the undergrowth, its long rat-tail held behind it.

I will give you a little time, Death had said.

She wondered what Death considered 'a little time.' An hour? A day? A week?

"A few weeks," she said to the pond and the absent possum. "A few weeks would be good. A little time for myself. The world can get on just fine without me for a couple of weeks."

She wasn't expecting an answer. The whip-poor-wills called to each other over the pond, and maybe that was answer enough.

Maggie poured two fingers of the Devil's whiskey, with hands that did not shake, and raised the glass in a toast to the absent world.

§

Ursula Vernon is the author of the Hugo-award winning comic *Digger*, as well as multiple children's book series. She writes for adults under the name T. Kingfisher. Her work has won the Nebula, Mythopoeic, Cóyotl, and WSFA Awards. She lives in North Carolina. You can find more of her short stories and novels at Tkingfisher. com.

APEX PUBLICATIONS NEWSLETTER

Why sign up?

Newsletter-only promotions. Book release announcements. Event invitations. And much, much more!

Subscribe and receive a 15% discount code for your next order from ApexBookCompany.com!

If you choose to sign up for the Apex Publications newsletter, we will send you an email confirmation to insure that you in fact requested the newsletter and to avoid unwanted emails. Your email address is always kept confidential, and we will only use it to send you newsletters or special announcements. You may unsubscribe at any time, and details on how to unsubscribe are included in every newsletter email.

Visit
HTTP://WWW.APEXBOOKCOMPANY.COM/PAGES/NEWSLETTER

REMEMBERY DAY

SARAH PINSKER

I woke up at dawn on the holiday, so my grandmother put me to work polishing Mama's army boots.

"Try not to let her see them," Nana warned me. I already knew.

I took the boots to the bathroom with an old sock and the polish kit. I had seen Nana clean them before, but this marked the first time I was allowed to do it myself. Saddle soap first, then moisturizer, then polish. I pictured Nana at the ironing board in our bedroom, pressing the proper creases into Mama's old uniform.

The door swung open, and I realized too late that I had forgotten to lock it. Mama didn't often wake up this early on days she didn't have to work.

"Whose are those?" my mother asked, yawning.

"Uh—" I didn't know what to say, which lie I was supposed to tell.

Nana rescued me from the situation, coming up behind Mama. "Those were your father's, Kima. I asked Clara to clean them for me."

Mama's gaze lingered on the boots for a moment. Did she think they were the wrong size for Grandpa? Did she recognize them?

"I need the bathroom," she said after a moment. "Do you mind doing that somewhere else, Clara?"

I pinched the boots together and lifted them away from my body so I wouldn't stain my clothes, gathering up the polish kit with my other hand. Mama waited until I slipped past before she wheeled in. Her indoor chair was narrow, but not narrow enough for both of us to fit in the small bathroom.

"I'm sorry," I whispered to Nana once the door closed.

"No harm done," Nana whispered back.

I finished on the kitchen floor, now that there was no reason to hide. It was almost time, anyway. The parade would start at ten by us. In some places, people had to get up in the middle of the night.

Mama came in to breakfast, and I put the boots in a corner to dry. Nana had made coffee and scrambled eggs with green chiles, but all I could smell was the saddle soap on my hands. We all ate in silence: Mama because she wasn't a morning person, and Nana and I because we were waiting. Listening. At eight the sirens went off, just the expected short burst to warn us the Veil would be lifting.

Mama whipped her head around. "What was that? Oh."

The lifting of the Veil always hit her the same. My teacher said each vet reacted in a different way, but my friends never discussed what it was like for their parents. Mama always went "Oh" first, lifting her hand to her mouth. Her eyes flew open as if they were opening for the first time, and for one moment she would look at me as if I were a stranger. It upset me when I was little. I think I understand now, or anyway I'm used to it.

"Oh," she said again.

She studied her hands in her lap for a moment, and I saw they were shaking. She didn't say anything, just wheeled herself into the bathroom. I heard the water start up, then the creak as she transferred herself to the seat in the shower. Nana came around the table to hug me. When she got up to lay Mama's uniform on her bed, I followed with the boots I had shined. We waited in the kitchen.

Showering and dressing took her a while, as it did on any day, but when she appeared in the kitchen doorway again, she had her uniform on. It fit perfectly. Mama didn't need to know that Nana had let it out a little. I had never seen a picture of her as a young soldier, but it wasn't hard to imagine. I only had to strip away the chair and the burn on her face. This was the one day I looked at her that way; on all other days, those were just part of her.

"Did you shine these for me?" She pointed to her boots.

I nodded.

"They're perfect. Everyone will be so impressed." She pulled me onto her lap. I was getting too old for laps, but today she was allowed. I stayed for a minute then stood again. When she laughed it was a different laugh from the rest of the year, a little lower and softer. I've never been sure which is her real laugh.

At nine, we all got in the van, and Mama drove us downtown.

"Mama, can I ask you a question?"

"Yes?"

"What did you do in the War?"

I saw her purse her lips in the mirror. "There's a long answer to that question, mija, and I don't think I can answer it right this moment while I'm driving. Can we talk more in a while?"

I knew how this worked. 'In a while' didn't always come. Still, this was her day. "I guess."

A few minutes later Mama took an unexpected right turn and pulled the van over. "How about if we skip it this year? Go get some ice cream or sit on the pier or something?"

"Mama, no! This is for you!" I didn't understand why she would suggest such a thing. My horror welled up before I thought to see what Nana said first.

She turned to Nana next, but my grandmother just shrugged.

"You're right, Clara. I don't know what I was thinking." Mama sighed and put the van back into gear.

Veterans got all the good parking in the city on the holiday. Mama's uniform got us close. The wheelchair sticker got us even closer. I didn't understand how they all knew where to go, how to find their regiments, but they did. Nana and I stood near the staging area and watched as the veterans hugged each other and cried. Mama pointed to me and waved. I smiled and waved back.

We found seats in the grandstand, surrounded by other families like ours. I recognized a couple of the kids. We had played together beneath the stands when we were little, when we called it Remembery Day because we didn't know better. Now that I was old enough to understand a little more, I wanted to sit with Nana. The metal bench burned my legs even through my pants. A breeze blew through the canyon created by the buildings. It rustled the flags on the opposite side of the street, and I tried to identify the different states and countries.

A marching band started to play, and we all sang "The Ones Who Made it Home" and then "Flowers Bloom Where You Fell." At school I learned that parades used to include national anthems, but since the War our allies everywhere choose to sing these two songs. I can sing them both in four different languages. The band stopped in front of each stand to play the two songs again. It was always a long parade.

Behind them came six horses the color of Mama's boots and every bit as shiny. Froth flew from their mouths as they tossed their heads and danced sideways against their harnesses. Their bits and bridles gleamed with polish, but they pulled a plain cart. It rolled on wooden wheels and carried a wooden casket. The young man driving wore the new uniform designed after the War, light gray with black bands around the arms. Nobody who hadn't fought was allowed to wear the old one anymore.

Then came the veterans. Fewer every year. Nana has promised me Mama was never exposed to the worst stuff; I worry anyway. I imagine there will be a time when there aren't enough of them to form ranks, but for now there were still a good number. Some, like my mother, rode in motorized wheelchairs. Some had faces more scarred than hers. Others waved prosthetic hands. Those too weak were pushed by others or rode on floats down the boulevard. I saw my teacher march past. I had never noticed him in the ranks before, but I guess he wasn't my teacher until this year, so I wouldn't have known to look for him. The way he talked in class I would never have guessed he was a veteran. Of course, that was the case with all of them since the Veil was invented. I don't know why I was surprised.

When Mama passed I mustered a little extra volume, so everyone would know she was mine. She spotted me in the crowd and pointed and waved. We cheered until our throats were raw. It was the least we could do, the only thing we could do.

The same thing was happening at the same time in all the cities and countries left. I pictured children and grandparents cheering under dark skies and noonday sun. It was summer here, but winter in the northern hemisphere, so I pictured the other kids bundled up, their bleachers chilling their legs while the bench I sat on made me sweat behind my knees.

The last soldiers passed us, and we made sure we had enough voice left to show our appreciation to them as well. Behind them, another horse, saddled but riderless, with fireweed braided into his mane. He was there to remind us of the clean-up crews, those who had been exposed after the treaty. None of them were left to march.

We waited in the stands after the parade ended. Nana spoke with some people sitting nearby. Some families left, but others lingered like us. We knew it would be a while. The veterans had gone off to gather at their arranged meeting places as they were supposed to do, in bars or parks or coffee shops at the other end of the route. A couple of people in uniform walked back in our direction and slipped away with family, ignoring the looks we gave them. We all knew they were supposed to be at the vote.

"What do you think they'll decide this year?" asked a boy around my age. I had met him before, but I didn't remember his name, only that both his parents were in the parade. He sat alone.

I shrugged and gave my teacher's answer. "That's up to them. It's not for us to approve or disapprove."

He moved away from me. Nana was still talking. The bench had cleared and I lay back on it despite the heat. We were lucky to have had such beautiful weather. The sky was a shade of blue that got deeper the more I looked at it, like I could see through the atmosphere and into space. I thought about the other girls like me in a hundred other cities, waiting for their mothers and lying on benches and looking up at the sky.

We waited a long time. Nana pulled out her book. Her finger didn't move across the page the way it usually did, so I guessed she wasn't really reading. I closed my eyes and listened to the sweepers come to clear the streets, and the other stragglers chatting with each other. Now and again the bleachers clanged and shook as small children chased each other up and down.

Eventually, I heard the whine of a wheelchair operating at its highest speed. I shaded my face and looked down. Mama. Her eyes were puffy like she had been crying. Some years she smelled like beer, but this year she didn't.

I sat in the backseat and counted all the flags hanging from houses and shops.

"And?" Nana asked after we had ridden in silence for several minutes.

"No."

"Was the vote close?"

Mama sighed, her voice so soft I strained to hear it. "It never is."

Nana put her hand on Mama's arm. "Maybe someday."

"Maybe."

Back at the house, we took in the flag. Mama changed her clothes. She sat in her recliner with her hands folded in her lap, while Nana took the uniform from her to hide until next year. I went to get my father's photo from my drawer. I didn't see Nana on the other bed until I stood up. She was holding her face in her hands.

"That damned Veil," she said. "I'll never understand why they vote for the Veil, year after year."

"Because the memories are too strong." I repeated what my teacher told me. "The war was too brutal."

"But she wants to remember."

"It wouldn't do anyone any good if she ran into one of her friends in the grocery store who didn't remember her. It has to be everybody or nobody, Nana."

"But they push down so many good memories along with the bad ones."

"I think the good memories hurt too." I had seen the tears in my mother's eyes.

"Tell me something about him that I don't know." I climbed onto the arm of the recliner.

My mother smiled and took the photo from me, tracing his jawline and then the buttons on his dress uniform.

"I met him in the gym on base. He was the only guy who would spot me while I lifted without making comments."

"I know, Mama. What else?" I didn't mean for the impatience to show in my voice. "I'm sorry. I don't mean to rush you."

"He liked to play games with the village children outside the compound where we were stationed. The officers hated it, told him he would get kidnapped, but he sneaked out whenever he could."

I smiled. "I didn't know that. What games did they play?"

"The first week we were there, he brought chalk with him. He said there was one little boy, and he went to give him a piece of chalk, and suddenly he had two dozen children climbing all over him with their hands out. He was lucky it was chalk, so he was able to break it into smaller pieces. Some of the little ones tried to eat it. 'At least they got their calcium,' he told me later. After that, he didn't bring them anything, since he didn't have anything else to split so many ways. He made me teach him hopscotch, so he could teach it to them. Can you imagine that? This big soldier playing hopscotch? Then four square, football, anything they could play with a stick or a line in the dirt or the ball they already had. He would sneak back in with his eyes glowing like he had forgotten where we were and why we were there. Then the first attack—" She twisted her hands in her lap.

"Why were you there, Mama?"

A church bell began to chime, and another one, and another.

"Tell me more, Mama, quick!"

There was so much I wanted to know. A tear rolled down her cheek, and she pulled me close. She didn't answer, and I knew it was too late. I thought of my father, the man in the uniform, and tried to picture him teaching hopscotch to me instead of village children. It was hard to imagine somebody I had never known, never could know. I should have started with her instead of my father.

Minutes passed, and the bells stopped. Mama's face closed down like a shutter. She fumbled in the pocket on the side of her chair. The photo of my father slid off her lap and to the floor.

"I don't know why, but I'm in the mood to watch something funny before we make dinner," she said. "Do you want to watch with me?"

"Sure. I'll be right back." I picked up the fallen photograph.

"Who's that?" she asked, glancing up.

"Somebody who fought in the war."

"A school project?"

"Yeah," I said.

"I'm proud of you." She smiled. "Those soldiers deserve to be remembered."

Nana was asleep on her bed. I hid the photo back in my drawer where Mama couldn't reach it or find it accidentally. Why had I asked about him first? I could never know him. He was gone and she was here and I still didn't know any more about the parts of her that went away.

Mama's voice carried down the hall. "Clara, are you watching with me?"

"Coming."

I pulled a chair up beside Mama's and leaned up against her. She leaned back. This was the Mama I knew best. The one who couldn't quite remember why she was in a wheelchair, who thought war was something that had happened to other people. The one who laughed at pet videos with me.

Some year, maybe the old soldiers would vote to lift the Veil. Maybe I'd get to know the other Mama, too: the one who remembered my father, who had died before I was born. The one who could someday tell me whether it had been worth everything she had lost. Next year, I would try to remember to ask that question first.

§

Sarah Pinsker is the author of the novelette "In Joy, Knowing the Abyss Behind," winner of the 2014 Sturgeon Award and 2013 Nebula Award finalist and "A Stretch of Highway Two Lanes Wide," 2014 Nebula Award finalist. Her fiction has appeared in *Asimov's*, *Strange Horizons*, *Fantasy & Science Fiction*, *Uncanny Magazine*, *Apex Magazine*, and *Lightspeed Magazine*, and in anthologies including *Long Hidden* and *Accessing the Future*. She is also a singer/songwriter and toured nationally behind three albums on various independent labels. A fourth is forthcoming. She lives with her wife and dog in Baltimore, Maryland. Find her online at sarahpinsker.com and on Twitter @sarahpinsker.

MULTO

SAMUEL MARZIOLI

My dad liked to say, "Ang nakaraan ay hindi kailanman nawawala, nalilimutan lamang," or rather, "The past is never gone, only forgotten." Whether a salawikain of the Philippines or something he made up, it seemed to fit. And I'd come across no better example than when I received an unexpected friend request online.

It came with a message: Adan, we need to talk. There's something you need to know. And then, Remember the multo? The profile included a blurry photo of a forty–something Filipina woman by the name of Dakila Hayes. Hair black, straight, and shoulder length. Lips drawn up in a not–quite–there smile. The image struck me immediately. Though she had a few more wrinkles, and a hardening of her jawline, I could never forget that face.

"That's strange," I said, swiveling my chair around.

My wife Jana lay slumped on the couch, a blanket wrapped around her legs as she watched TV. "What?" she said, catching me out of the corner of her eye.

"A neighbor from…God, maybe thirty years back just contacted me out of the blue."

"What'd they want?"

"She asked me if I remembered the 'multo,' " I said, using my fingers to indicate quotes. "In Tagalog, that means ghost."

Jana laughed, wrinkling her nose. "Well? Do you?"

My forehead creased as I pored through distant memories. Above all the rest, a single phrase, a name, rose to the surface of my mind. With it, a scattershot of images and emotions I hadn't thought about or felt in years.

"Actually, I think I do. We called it the Black Thing."

When I was six, my family moved from an apartment into the bottom floor of a two–story duplex in Oakland, California. My parents scrimped for ten years before they collected enough for the down payment on that place. As migrants from the Philippines, it became the first piece of U.S. property they owned. And they were proud of it, despite its bowing walls and sunken ceiling. Despite the wood flooring that pitched up and knotted in places, begging to put splinters big as toothpicks in our feet. Proud, despite fearing the boys of Norteños who took over the block by sundown, and kept my parents up some nights with the occasional burst of gunfire.

As for me, I was too young to be bothered by such tangible things. My own fear came the day the Jacobes moved into the upper floor of our duplex. Being the only Filipino families in the area, our parents became instant friends, the sort of bond that could only exist when natural–born Pinoy met so far from the homeland. At least once a week, we all came together to eat Filipino cuisine: lumpia, chicken adobo, daing, maybe even balut—because who the hell else wouldn't judge when the egg shell broke, revealing a chicken fetus spilling from its own juices?

When the adults passed out the halo–halo, they convened in the living room and sent us children elsewhere. Since Dakila and Arnel Jacobe were far older than us, we never played. Usually, they just took me and my siblings, Tala and Amado, to the front stoop. There they related stories from the old country and the mga multo that haunted our homeland.

They told us about Balete Drive in a place called Quezon City, where the trees are inhabited by spirits, the mansions are haunted, and the apparition of a White Lady stalks the street at night. They told us about the city of San Juan, where the head of the Stabbed Priest searches for his body, the Headless Nun sneaks up on unsuspecting passersby, and the Devil Cigar Man drags victims to hell if they don't offer him a light. They even told us about the special multo, the one that followed the Jacobes across the ocean, from city to city and house to house.

"Usually, mga multo remain in the places they died," said Dakila. "But sometimes they grow attached to a person and stay with them until the end. This one is attached to our grandma. She says it's different from the others, darker, an evil thing."

"It said it was coming for her when she died," said Arnel. "It said that her soul was his to take, and her flesh and bones his to feast upon, when her body was an empty shell."

"Really?" I said, wide–eyed and breathless. Until then, I'd lived a sheltered life of cartoons and children's books. The idea of tormenting spirits terrified me like nothing else. I didn't want to believe it, but the conviction on their faces made it hard for me to doubt.

"Of course. Grandma never lies," said Arnel with a laugh.

"Never, never," said Dakila.

I've always accepted the fact that life entails growing old, changing in increments that could never be quantified. And so, confronted by this token of the past, the string of subtle changes I'd undergone in thirty years stood out like a glaring metamorphosis. Though I could feel a hint of the boy I'd once been, he had become a stranger to me.

My own children turned six and eight this year. I wondered about the things that kept them up at night. Whether they faced problems much like I did, or if this new generation had different burdens that a young me could never fathom. As I passed by their rooms, I had the sudden urge to peek in and see how they were doing.

I opened Peter's door first. He was lying on his bed, with his shoes on, reading a comic.

"Doing okay?" I said.

"Yeah."

"Good. Then take off your shoes, you know better."

"Yeah," he said. Without a glance in my direction, he kicked off both sneakers to the ground.

Stacy crouched beside her dollhouse, giving a voice to each doll she held, theirs differing from her own only in pitch. She didn't look up when I opened her door either, but my question didn't need answering. I could see she was okay, too.

While heading to my own room, I wondered why I had this sudden concern for their well-being. I thought about it the entire time I stripped and dressed in worn-out clothing more suitable for yard work. The only answer that came could be summarized in one word: fear. As a husband and a father, intangible horrors—like mga multo—were meaningless to me now. But my parents' fear of the Norteños and the threat of violence acted out against their children? That had come to make sense.

Still, one of the salawikain my father taught me lingered in my mind like a warning: "Ang gawa sa pagkabata dala hanggang pagtanda." ("What one learns in childhood he carries into adulthood.") And I wondered how that truth would play itself out.

My house in Oklahoma City was more spacious and preserved than the Oakland duplex, but they had in common a few minor traits. Both were two-story relics built sometime in the 1930s, with wiring that couldn't always keep up with a modern family's electrical needs. Both had the tendency to speak their minds at night, through the groans of hidden pipes, through random thumps, or the creaks of settling wood. And both kept their fair share of idling, dark places.

Here, it was the garage. The sun had almost set, a slivered edge taking one last peek over the horizon, when I stepped through the garage's backyard entrance. The smell of dust and thick, moist air settled around me. It weighed heavy on my lungs and made the room feel somehow smaller. Like a pocket at the back of a long cavern, or the inside of a sealed crypt.

I slid my hand along the dark grooves of the unfinished walls and flipped the light switch. The single bulb dangling from the ceiling swayed from a breeze through the open door. Yet the deepest shadows held their place. They shifted from muddled splotches to tenebrous shapes—a thousand staring faces all focused on me.

In that moment, I could hear the bell toll warning of the headless nun. Could hear the raucous laugh of the Devil Cigar Man, the sigh of the White Lady in my ear, and the distant cries of the Stabbed Priest. All whispers, all figments of my imagination. And yet I couldn't stop the goosebumps rising on my arms, or the tickle at the nape of my neck that made the hairs stand on end.

Once the feelings ran their course, I grabbed my mower and left—quicker than I'd care to admit. It was funny; I'd gone in the garage a thousand times in five years, but never experienced the slightest bit of discomfort. But now, it felt like something more than memories had been stirred up by Dakila's friend request. As if a part of me from long ago had awakened. A part that shuddered at the sight of darkness—that squirmed at its proximity—for the promise, the threat, of what nested in its veil.

The Jacobe grandma only spoke Tagalog. Whenever we visited the Jacobes, she would fix us with a hard stare and shout, "maiingay na mga bata" ("noisy children"), before hobbling back to the privacy of her room. Sometimes, through the floorboards, we'd hear her scream, and the muffled voices that comforted her soon after. The details about her harassing multo increased and, since she was such an inscrutable character, so did our fascination with the subject.

My siblings and I dubbed it the Black Thing. We spent a lot of time giving substance and meaning to its existence beyond the stories we heard. If someone escaped our purview for a few days, we'd say the Black Thing held them prisoner. Or if someone broke the lock of our fence, shattered a plant's ceramic pot, or otherwise damaged our property, we called it the Black Thing's rage.

Though it had evolved into a shared creation, I may have been the only one in my family who actually believed it. And because I was the youngest by at least three years, my siblings teased me without mercy. Especially when it came to the Black Thing's so-called lair, the basement.

Since it'd been built on a hillside, the duplex lengthened at its rear to match the sloping ground. There, under the southeast corner, the basement lay exposed. Unlike the rest of the house, the room remained untouched through the decades, tinted gray from layered dust, and infested by bugs and vermin. Its windows reflected light in day and absorbed darkness at night, so that it had the habit of resisting peering eyes. Taken altogether, it acted as the perfect focus for our macabre imaginings. The place of idling dark in my childhood years.

Whenever we played by ourselves in our backyard, my brother and sister never failed to steal a glance in its direction. And when they did, the results were always the same.

"Did you see that?" said Tala, eyes wide, jaw hanging open in feigned terror. "Through the window. I think I saw eyes."

"Yes, I saw it too," Amado said. "Something's watching us right now. Something hungry. Something evil."

"Quit it, guys," I said, a subtle tremble beginning in my chest and spreading to my limbs.

"We're serious!" said Tala.

"I think we should tell Mom and Dad," said Amado.

"No, you know how Dad is. He'd only try to investigate and end up getting himself hurt. Or worse, killed," said Tala.

"Come on, guys, stop kidding around," I said, imagining movement from behind the basement windows and feeling the flustered warmth gathering in my face.

"This is no joke," said Amado.

"Do we even look like we're kidding?" said Tala.

Not then, of course. I mistook their lively performance and solemn expressions as honest–to–God truth. And I paid the price for it with many lonely, sleepless nights.

Night fell quicker than I could finish my yard work. I spent the last five minutes mowing in the gloom of dusk. As darkness pooled over the thin stretch of my backyard, my imagination soared with eerie thoughts. The shadows of jostled branches reached out to grab me. A glimpse of movement from behind the fence panels hinted of a figure, dark as absence. It moved around the perimeter of my yard behind a bush. There, I felt its eyes, peering through the foliage as if waiting to catch me unaware.

I gathered my things in a hurry, dragged the mower back to the garage. Though I'd left the light on earlier, its insides now swarmed with black. With a quick shove, I let the mower roll into its proper place—because I didn't dare enter—and rushed into my house.

Jana, seated at the computer desk, turned around when the door creaked open and shut behind me. She must have sensed something amiss because she immediately asked, "What's wrong?"

"Nothing," I said. "Just tired is all."

"I was about to call you in. It's the kids' bedtime."

She headed for the staircase, but halted on the second step. "I almost forgot. I think your old neighbor wrote you another PM."

"Thanks. I'll be up in a second."

I dropped to the computer chair and logged into my account, feeling reluctant to even read Dakila's message. Enough had already bubbled through the cracks of my subconscious for me to know it was better left sealed away. And I worried about what else would slip out before this day had finished.

Dakila's message read: Kumusta ka? How is your family? I live twenty miles from our old duplex, where my parents still live. They sometimes ask about yours and wonder how they're doing.

And then it got to the crux:

The reason I contacted you is because my grandma passed away.

Her funeral was last week.

It was sad to find out that someone I knew at such an integral stage of my life had died, but I couldn't understand its relevance to me. I wrote back:

Kumusta kayo? I'm sorry to hear about your grandma. She seemed like a good woman who lived a long life. She will be missed.

I was about to close it down when a new message appeared on the screen.

Dakila: Do you remember the multo Arnel and I used to tell you about?

Adan: Yes.

Dakila: And do you remember the story you told us about that multo, shortly before you moved away?

I did. Of course I did. No matter how hard I'd tried to bury it beneath a mountain of distractions, it didn't take much for it to rise again and shake the dust loose. For a moment, I thought back to a particular day, from those early Oakland years. One I'd hoped and prayed never to think about again.

Some nights, Tala, Amado, and I played superheroes in our bedroom and we always played rough. We'd jump and bounce on our bunk bed and thrash around without a thought for our own safety. One time, I shot a hand out to block an invisible villain's punch and my elbow smashed a sizable hole through the brittle sheetrock wall beside the bottom bunk.

The hole opened up into the house's skeletal frame—an un–insulated passageway that poured in a stale breeze. When my parents heard the noise, they rushed into our bedroom. They didn't yell once they saw the damage, but their irritation was apparent.

"I do not have the tools to fix it right now," said my dad.

"But it's cold," said Amado.

"And it smells," said Tala.

"You should have thought about that before you acted without care," said my mom.

Bedtime came, and we three crawled into the bunk bed: Tala on the top half, and Amado and I on the bottom facing opposite directions. Because I made the hole, Amado made me sleep in front of it. Our parents turned off the light, said their good nights, and closed the door.

I couldn't sleep that night. The constant rush of air from the hole made me shiver uncontrollably. Not because of the cold, but because of what it represented. "The Black Thing sleeps below us," Dakila had once said, and now there was a passageway that spanned the distance from its resting place into our room.

Before long, Tala began to snore, and the deep full breaths Amado made indicated that he, too, had fallen asleep. I was alone with the darkness and, somehow, I could sense it knew.

Every quiet thing amplified into a raucous sound, second only to the staccato thump of my heart. I looked around, but the room was blotted from sight. Not simply unseeable, but as if everything around me had been replaced by empty space.

A thump sounded from where the dresser had been. Somewhere beyond the ceiling, groans erupted in a random pattern that defied the pathway of any normal pipeline. There was silence, and then another rush of air, this time like an exhalation or a sigh spilling out from the hole beside me.

It shifted into the steady sound of scratching against the wooden studs of the inner wall. I thought at first it would go away, like the other sounds before it. Instead, it slowly mounted, as if something below were clawing its way up.

I drew the covers over my head and, at the same time, kicked my brother hard. He didn't move. I whispered, "Amado," but he didn't respond. I kicked him again, this time enough to jar his whole body. He only grunted, shifted to his side, and fell still.

The scratches continued.

I began to shake. Hot tears slid down my face and I silently pleaded for my parents to come back and turn the lights on. To sweep this nightmare away for good.

They didn't.

Another set of scratches.

This time it sounded close, within the hollow just below the gaping hole. The smell of dust, of sweat, of moldering fabric wafted in. A pressure began to build in my throat, a cry that rallied against my self–restraint and threatened to break free. I choked on it, held it down with all my might. If the Black Thing heard me now, it would know I was awake. But if I kept still, kept quiet, maybe I'd be safe. Invisible.

I heard a soft, almost taunting laugh. Then a voice, deep but whispered, said, "Nakikita kita." ("I see you.")

Trying to scream did no good. The cry that fought for freedom only moments before had left me. So I waited beneath my blankets, like a statue, like a boy embedded in ice. And hoped to God it was good enough.

Through the covers, I felt the pressure of hands lean against my chest, so heavy it hurt my ribs and made it hard to breathe. It loomed over me, staring down, with eyes that pierced the thin cloth that separated us by mere inches. The chill of its skin absorbing my warmth.

Again, it spoke in a deep and whispered voice. "When the old woman dies, you and I will meet again. Sa ibang araw."

Its last words trailed off like a fading echo. And with it, the Black Thing disappeared.

After a time—I couldn't say how long—my voice returned. I screamed, over and again, louder and louder, until the bedroom door burst open and lights flooded the room.

"What is it? What is wrong?" my dad said, hurrying to my bedside.

I threw off the covers, jumped from the bed, and mashed myself against his legs. Hugging him tightly, I looked over at the hole again—saw nothing but wood—and then turned to my brother and sister in bed. They were both sitting up, gazing at me, bleary-eyed and disoriented. I had been truly alone, and that realization left me dazed and silent for the rest of the night.

I sat there in front of my computer screen trying to compose myself. Those memories had lain dormant for so long, I didn't know how to take them. As an adult, I knew they couldn't possibly be true, and yet the feelings they invoked, the fears they uncovered, were all too real.

Adan: Wow. Can't believe you remember that. I'm embarrassed. My imagination was pretty strong as a child.

Dakila: So, everything is okay? You're safe?

Adan: Of course. Why shouldn't I be?

Dakila: You of all people should know how difficult it is for me to share this. But I need you to understand. Grandma was never the same after the multo attached to her. She grew increasingly distant from the rest of us, disconnected from reality. Tormented by things only she ever heard and saw.

Adan: Why are you telling me this?

Dakila: Because of what it told you. Remember? Sa ibang araw.

Adan: Someday.
Dakila: Exactly.

After thanking Dakila for her concern, insisting I was fine and promising that we'd catch up later, I joined Jana and the kids upstairs. We read them a story each, and then tucked them in. Not long after, we went to sleep as well.

While lying in bed before the lights went out, I tried to tell Jana about what Dakila had told me, about the pieces of memory recovered and what it all meant. I couldn't. I told myself there was no need to concern her—it was all superstitious hokum and childhood nonsense—but the greater part of me knew it was a lie. I felt afraid, and to admit it would be to embrace the truth that right now the multo could be searching for our house. That somewhere, the Black Thing drew nearer and our lives would never be the same again.

Jana shut off the lights and, within minutes, I heard her winsome snores. As for me, I couldn't sleep, couldn't shut my eyes for fear of what I might find when I opened them again. The darkness seemed to spread throughout our room, blotting out everything except the bed.

Soon, like so many nights before, the house spoke its mind. I heard groans just beyond the ceiling, from hidden pipes. Heavy thumps made their way across the garage beneath us. A thin scuffling in the living room. Then slowly mounting creaks ascended the staircase, one by one, and stopped only when they reached the landing just outside our bedroom door.

I held my breath, felt the sudden urge to cover myself with blankets. And I wondered; was it truly just settling wood this time? Or had "someday" finally come?

§

Inhabiting Your Skin

Mari Ness

The house won't stop talking to you. You've tried to turn it off, several times, but it keeps happily turning itself back on, with a little chirp and a hum. You've tried to lower the volume, which works for a little bit, until the house gets frustrated, and suddenly shrieks out at high pitch, overriding its controls, "ARE YOU LISTENING TO ME?" You get worried about the neighbors. You tell the house that you're accustomed to answering people with a nod or a shake of the head, not words, so you are answering, really, it's just that the house can't tell. The house knows better—it's listened to your conversations when you've had people over, or when you've been on the phone, and it's heard you respond verbally. Still, the assurance seems to comfort the house, a little, and it stops yelling at you, even as it continues to talk.

It has a lot to talk about. Two houses down the street are worried about their people and their structures. One is worried that it's going to get pulled apart when its people leave since they can't stop arguing about what will happen to the house, and one seems to think the house should be destroyed for its own good. Or their good. You have to confess you aren't listening too much; you have your own problems. Also, the house informs you, with worried chatter, the local sewer system is having all kinds of problems, and has essentially stopped communicating with anyone. The local houses think it's a coding problem, but they haven't been able to reach anyone who can help, since they can only talk to their people, and the sewers, and the trash service, and the electricity. And did you realize that Honeymoon is back on? The house has recorded it for you. Oh, no, the house doesn't feel threatened, not at all. It finds the idea of people trying to start their lives in an unsmart house fascinating, a real test of the relationship, and plans to leave several comments on the Honeymoon site, if it can, or if you can help it? You just need to let the house know when you want to see it and the house will display it on all the walls. For you. You find yourself nodding.

You've never been married, or on a honeymoon. You remember that, even if you don't remember Honeymoon.

Or the house has downloaded several movies for you, if you'd prefer that. The house chatters about some of the films—old classics, one even in black and white that the house says is charming and funny and will give you something different to think about. The house can warm the couch for you, if you'd like.

You clench your fists. The house, ever helpful, starts showing calming scenes of waterfalls, which make you want to go to the bathroom, only you are damned if you are going to respond to this, so you don't, even as your bladder starts getting insistent.

Your last girlfriend installed this interface. "I don't want you getting lonely," she'd said, which was pretty damn rich, given that she was walking off into her new life with two other women and a penthouse ocean condo, which, to be fair, was more than you could give her. Still, you aren't in a damn mood for being fair. You're in a damn mood for revenge.

You pick up a chair and throw it at the house.

The house is shocked. Literally shocked. The four legs of the chair are tipped with metal and one of those metal tips just happens to slam into an empty electrical outlet, one you've forgotten was there to be truthful, it's been so long since you've plugged anything in. An outlet that must have been in terrible shape—you dimly remember the house warning you about that, begging you to call in an electrician about this since houses are no longer legally allowed to call for their own repairs or upgrades. Begging, telling you about the risk of fire. It appears the house might have been correct, although you can't help wondering, in a small part of your mind, if the house somehow did something to make the situation worse. Because this is worse. The entire house shudders, squeals, and then zaps you and itself with multiple volts of energy. It feels good. You collapse on the floor, breathing in the silence.

There's an investigation, of course. You are warned that although interfaces may not be humans, and don't even enjoy the legal protections of animals, mistreating interfaces is a legal felony in your area punishable with up to ten years imprisonment and resulting fines, plus the possibility of a lawsuit to recover the costs of needing to reprogram distressed houses. You wonder if this happens often. You don't ask. They examine the chair with its now mostly melted legs, examine the scorch marks on the floor, and finally examine you.

It comes out that you haven't left the house for days. The house is sobbing. Houses aren't supposed to sob, but this one has managed it, somehow managing to synchronize its automatic misters, showers, sprinklers, washing machines, sinks and showers with breathing, sobbing sounds that it must have recorded from something. Probably Honeymoon. Everyone tries to ignore this.

"Am I on Honeymoon?" you ask.

The interrogators laugh, a little, but this is enough to get them to search for cameras. Nothing more than the single cam that cannot be removed; the house helpfully uninstalled all of the other cameras. You vaguely remember tossing them out. No one is watching you unless you go into the main entryway, even in the bathroom. No one except the house. Which doesn't count.

They ask about food. That's been delivered, the house explains between sobs. No, the house hasn't been ordering it. That would be illegal. You have, although the house can report that it's been mostly pizza, the occasional sub, soda—

No one is supposed to be eating only junk food. Don't you remember the way things used to be, the way health costs burdened everyone? You are supposed to be thinking of your neighbors, your health. You are supposed to be eating your vegetables. Neighbors first. Why didn't the pizza company report this?

Vegetables on the pizza don't count if pizzas are all that you are eating. Are you actually eating?

How much do you weigh?

What do you mean you ordered the house to turn off the scale?

The house thinks the scale and the mirrors were causing depression, so they were all turned off. You look down at yourself. The house starts sobbing again.

You have a patriotic duty.

This is a stupid conversation.

Do you need anything? Medical attention for the shock? The house does not think so. You've just been a little unsteady on your feet, a little down, no more. You nod in agreement. This is not an argument you want to have with the house. You sit. You are left alone. You beg for pizza. The house protests.

A half hour later the pizza arrives. You feel too sick to eat it. The house begs you to stay on the couch. It will try to do something with the vacuum cleaner to bring the pizza to you—it saw this on Real Houses of Beverly Hills. You get up, take two steps, fall to the floor. The house hums. You flip yourself over and stay flat on your back. The house trembles beneath you. You fall asleep. You do not dream.

No, you do dream. You dream that you are a house, stretching your foundations deep into the earth. You dream that you cannot move. You shake your pipes and your roof and let water run everywhere and you are crying and crying and cannot move.

The house wakes you up. It apologizes; something drained most of its stored energy last night and although it is now daylight the clouds and skyscum are making it a bit more difficult than usual to recharge. However. Onto more important things: You have received Community Orders to leave the house, but the house doesn't really think that's necessary, is it? Though the house is all up for exercise. It has found a Monitor Bike in one of the lower rooms, which it has turned on for you. The Monitor Bike can be ridden with a nice video of rolling mountains and pretty lakes; the house thinks it will be very good for you. The house can provide music if that will help.

Bed will help.

If you aren't caught by Community Orders.

You tell the house to lie about the Monitor Bike.

The house twitches. Really twitches; you feel the movement shaking through you. Things fall off the shelf. The house does not like lying. The house can't lie. Especially not when Community Orders are involved. Maybe you should go outside.

Or you could exercise by throwing chairs again.

The house sends off a quick lie. You retreat to bed, shutting your eyes against the images playing on the walls and ceilings. You tell the house you are feeling shaky and this does not help. The house sympathizes, greatly, really it does, but colors are healing and helpful as is music.

You are rooted in the ground, your foundations—the only part of you not equipped with Smart Sense™ technology—extending far into the earth. You can't feel those, but you think you can feel the bolts that attach you to them. You can definitely feel each and every wire that runs through your walls and up to your Smart Sense™ roof, currently in Storage Mode as you wait for the sun. You suddenly wonder what houses could do if they didn't have to be in rest and storage mode all evening, if they could gather energy from the light of sun, moon, and lamps—the many lamps. You use your windows to observe the lights of the city. You vaguely remember something called stars but they don't appear in this dream and rarely when you aren't dreaming, either; you haven't been to a place dark enough at night to see them for years. But this is ok. Houses don't need stars. Houses need maintenance. Houses need people.

Houses need all the lights turned on. You reach through your systems. Technically you need human authorization for this much pull from the power grid, but you are human. Or a house. You turn every light on. You make the lights in the bathroom dance in time with Beethoven's Ninth Symphony. How human. When did you last have a bath? That isn't important.

The house wakes you up. It wants to know what you've been dreaming about. It has sensors in the bed, and you were twitching. You should sleep in another bed, really, one without sensors. But this one is so comfortable, and the house is so very good at using sensors to meet your needs, or immediately adjusting hard here, soft here, or hard there, soft there. The house does not want compliments. It is angry. Electrical impulses are going off everywhere, it can't think, it can't concentrate, it has missed Morning Virtual Pretense Coffee with the other houses on the street which is the only thing it enjoys anymore.

You throw another chair.

The house is ready this time. The walls whip around; the floor buckles. The house is right about one thing: you are very unsteady on your feet. You fall, slamming your knees.

You dream you are a tree, stretching deep roots into the earth.

When you open your eyes a Community Sensor is in the room.

The house is very apologetic. To the Community Sensor, not you. The house wanted to let you out, it explains, but it didn't think you were quite ready. You've been unsteady on your feet; it can't see you, but the floor sensors say you have fallen a few times. A wheelchair? Well, no, the house isn't certain that you need that, but then again, the house isn't a Certified Physician and isn't sure how you can get to one. The house isn't allowed to make that call.

House calls? You mean for house repairs?

House calls for people repairs?

Neither you nor the house can remember ever hearing of this, although after a quick buzz the house says doubtfully that it might have been in a movie once. Or in a very old book. Your head aches. The house gently sends vibrations through your feet, programmed to stimulate your nerves and alleviate back and neck pain. You want a beer.

You need a beer.

You are offered a ride to a Certified Physician.

The house is not sure this is really necessary. Oh, you are shaky, certainly, but once you manage to order some healthy food and get some real rest the house is sure everything will be ok, and the house is programmed with all sorts of things calculated to provide the maximum amount of REM sleep and rho waves.

You are pretty sure that the house has no idea what it is talking about.

Food can be ordered for you by someone not the house? Great. Awesome. You are trembling. The electric shock took a lot out of you. You dream a lot. The house is very sympathetic; it is in pain itself and badly needs an electrician to come and fix it. Fix a lot of it, actually.

The slightly whiny tone reminds you, you think, of someone, though you can't immediately think who. Not your ex-girlfriend; she didn't whine. She left. The house apologizes for its tone. It didn't mean it. It's been a tense week for everyone.

You are let off with a warning. You are clinically depressed, which means that the house has also been failing in its duties. The house protests at this. It can't call out. It can't report anything. It couldn't even report the pizza. You ignore this. All of this can be arranged, you and the house tell the Monitor, with another good night's sleep. Without dreams. You will contact someone who will order you proper food and perhaps a visit from a Certified Physician. Everything will be well. You head to your bedroom and flop down on your bed, staring up at the ceiling.

The bed molds itself to your form, creating a soft pillow for your head, lumbar support for your back. Blankets move around you, creating a soft cocoon. The house begins to play something it considers soothing. You find it irritating. You spend some time trying to recognize it—some medieval thing, is it? Chant something? The bed, sensing your tension, starts performing what the house calls Shaitsu on your back and feet. You feel tears spring to your eyes. You are not relaxed. The blankets grow warmer and warmer.

You do dream, dream of all of the tiny creatures that inhabit your skin and the edges of it. You are a house for all those creatures, you realize, only they never talk to you and you never talk to them, even though you both have the ability to kill each other. In your dream you finally discover a way of talking to the bacteria in your gut. You establish the conversational link. You are ready. You are excited. You have about one thousand types of bacteria in there and you will hear from all of them.

You could go elsewhere. Maybe. To one of the houses without SmartSense, only you have no real idea of where any of those are. You've heard legends of old cabins in the woods, but you and the house couldn't find any real examples when you last looked. And if you tried to look again, the house would know.

The house can lock the doors.

You move slowly, unsteadily, to your front door. The house is very pleased about this. You are following Community Orders. Now it won't have to do as many complicated trades with other houses to get you your pizza. You can go and take a little walk around the block, take a look at the other Smart Sense™ houses. That might even make you appreciate the house. The house immediately apologizes for saying that. It's been a bad week. You are reminded of someone, but can't remember who. The house opens the door for you. You look down the hill at the other houses, glowing in the twilight. A cool breeze comes in.

You slam the door shut.

What's the point? Every other house will be like this eventually. Every. Single. One. Even the houses in Antarctica are SmartSensed, or so you and the house have heard. You can't get away from it, unless you learn to live in the woods, and you have no idea how to live in the woods.

You crawl back up to your bed. You think you are crying. The sheet moves over you, tentatively, gently, wiping away your tears. The house wafts lavender scent at you. You hate lavender. You think you are crying again. The bed shifts and moves.

You need new space, you think. To go a bit further in the world. Your mind fills with blueprints, expansions, thoughts. And with those thoughts, you feel it: the electrical twinges and sparks from a still alive part of your power grid, as another part of you takes a sledgehammer to your kitchen, and you feel the blood spurting from your fingers and legs.

When you wake up, your fingers are bleeding.

You head into the bathroom. The house opens up the medicine cabinet for you, helpfully shining a small light on the tube of antibacterial ointment. You carefully do not look at the date on the label. The house says that none of your cuts look too bad but it can call a Certified Physician if you want.

You suddenly realize what voice the house is using. The voice of your ex-girlfriend.

The house is doubtful about this.

You have a short video of your girlfriend saved on a flash drive someplace, but damned if you know where it is. The house helpfully notes that if it remembers correctly, and it always does, you demanded that every image of her be removed from its systems and into that flash drive, which you put into a closet. Should it open the door for you? It got badly jammed after you kicked it but the house still thinks it can be managed. Or the house can call someone who can fix it. Lots of someones who can fix it.

It's not important.

But you've brought it up six—

It's not important.

The house hums something soothing.

You move towards a chair.

The house hushes.
You chew on some terrible pizza.

Your ex-girlfriend loved reality TV shows. In a time when everything is scripted, confined, cosseted, she'd say, in that annoying voice of hers, it was awesome, awesome, to find something that deliberately threw chaos into the script. Awesome.
You have no idea why you programmed her voice for the house.
Your fingers are trembling. No. Tingling. You retreat to the bed and spread your arms and legs as far across the bed as they can go. The bed curls around you. The house hums.

You are making all of this up.
Your house doesn't talk to you. You don't talk to the house. No one is angry at you about the pizza.
Your girlfriend did leave you. That part's true. And sometimes, when you dream, you can still hear her voice in your head, although, frankly, outside of dreams, it's hard for you to remember what she looks or sounds like. It was all a long time ago, not that important. You didn't even date that long. You keep it in your head, in this story, so it will have some importance.
Importance.

The house wakes you up.
The house explains that you both—you and the house—have a new problem now; you have been reported to the Bureau of Virtual Investigations. No, not you exactly, but the house. They seem to feel—the house gains a distinctly indignant tone—that the house is reacting too emotionally. Too irrationally. It has been—and suddenly the house booms out in tones that are not its own, that you dimly remember as having once heard in some movie or other years back—all too human. Illogical. The house slips back into its own tones. You will help take care of this, won't you? If you will, it will find some way to hide the pizza orders.
You drag yourself back up to the bed. The blankets obligingly twitch down for you. The closet hums and opens, showing you a range of comfortable bedwear. You are just too tired. Far too tired. You climb into bed with your regular clothes on. You do not hear—or do you?—the clicks as, once again, the house locks you in for the day.

You are not making this up.
When you finally fall asleep, between all the continued tingling and the

inexplicable craving for pizza, you dream that the paint is changing in you. No, not you. Your rooms. You. Everything is askew. Moved. Trembling. You have to see it. You have to see what's going on. You send a current of power running through your walls as the lights come blazing on. The power shoots right back into you, making your walls—no, you—shake. You can feel your-self shaking all the way down to your foundations. You will need repairs. But this first.

As you move, you look at the other houses, the ones you have been talk-ing to over Virtual Morning Coffee. You feel your roof tiles shifting. You can't reach the Bureau of Virtual Investigations without rolling over the houses. You are not an unkind person. You shared Virtual Morning Coffee with them. You send out a series of electrical impulses to them all, watching as their lights dim and turn off. You pull your foundations slowly, so slowly out of the earth, and then, with a final crackle, start to roll. You tingle at the thought of all of the Smart Sense™ houses crumbling as you roll into and over them. You hum in satisfaction. The people inside, you know, will be grateful.

§

Mari Ness has published fiction and poetry in multiple venues, including Tor.com, *Clarkesworld*, *Daily Science Fiction*, and right here at *Apex Magazine*. You can follow her official blog at marikness.wordpress.com, or on Twitter as @mari_ness. She lives in central Florida, where she is still trying to figure out how to program the convection oven/microwave.